W9-CMY-338

The Prince
who wrote a letter

Written by Ann Love

Illustrated by Toni Goffe

Ann Love's royalties are donated to Cancer Research.

THE BRYANT LIBRARY
2 PAPER MILL ROAD
ROSLYN, N.Y. 11576-2193

Published by Child's Play (International) Limited
Swindon   New York   Bologna   Toronto   Sydney
Illustrations © Toni Goffe 1992   ISBN 0–85953–398–0 (hard cover)   Printed in Singapore
                                         ISBN 0–85953–399–9 (soft cover)

Once, there were two kings.
They lived in two castles
on opposite sides of a valley.

On this side is the castle
of kind King Clifford.

On this side is the castle
of good King Rudolf.

In one of the castles
lived a prince
whose name was Paul.

One day, he went to school
for the very first time.

When he came home, his father King Clifford said:
"What did you do in school today?"

"I had to write a letter," Prince Paul replied.

The King was amazed.

"You wrote a letter!?" he exclaimed.
"On your very first day at school!?"

The King hurried to tell the Queen.

"The Prince wrote a letter in school today!" said the King.

The Queen was very pleased . . .

"To whom did he write, Dear?" she asked.

"I don't know, Dear," replied the King. "I forgot to ask.
But I expect he wrote to his very best friend, Prince Peter."

Prince Peter lived in the castle on the opposite side of the valley.

The Queen hurried off to tell the Queen Mother . . .

The Queen Mother was most surprised.

"What did he write in the letter?" she asked.

"I do not know," replied the Queen.
"But I am sure he must have written
something very nice!"

"Of course," agreed the Queen Mother.
"Prince Paul would only write
a nice, sensible letter.

Not like some people,
who might write a silly letter . . ."

"Yes," said the Queen. "Some people might write:

'Dear Prince Peter,
I hope your father, King Rudolf, is keeping well,
because I think he's getting much too fat!'"

The Queen Mother laughed.
She knew the Queen was only joking, but secretly
she also thought that King Rudolf was getting too fat.
The Queen Mother was no spring chicken herself.

The Queen Mother's maid overheard the conversation.

She knew it was rude to eavesdrop,
so she only listened with one ear,
and she did not hear exactly what had been said.

She couldn't wait to tell her friend, the castle cook.

"Mabel! Mabel!" she called, as she ran down the stairs
to the kitchen. "You'll never believe what has happened!"

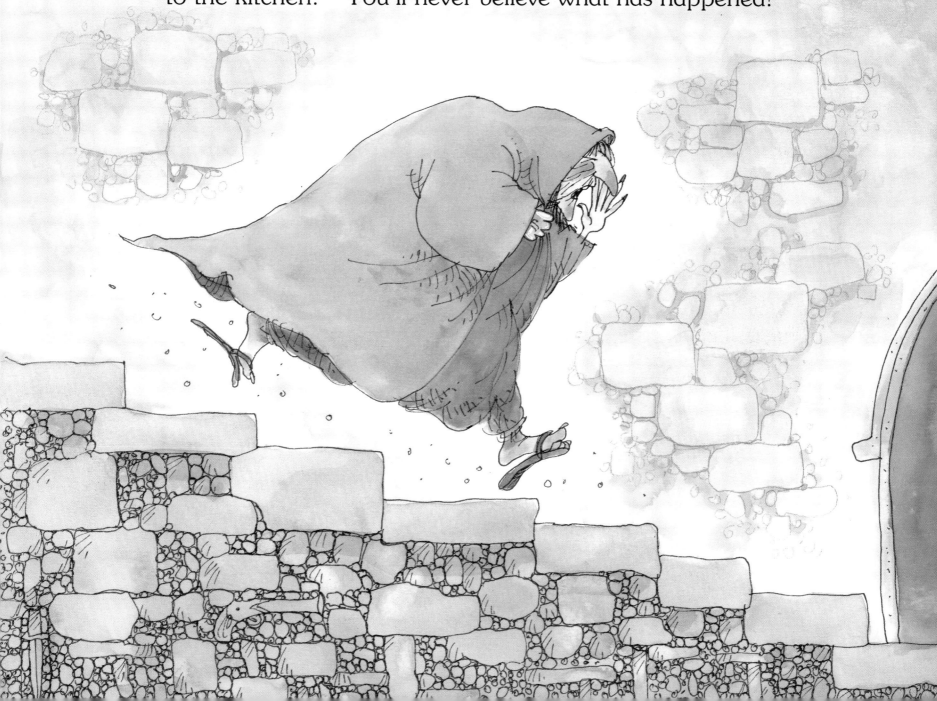

The maid repeated the conversation she thought she had heard.

"Prince Paul has written a letter to his friend, Prince Peter.
He has told him that he thinks King Rudolf is a fat old thing."

The castle cook was most alarmed.

"Oh!" she cried. "What a rude boy! When King Rudolf hears about the letter, he will become very angry."

She hurried off to tell her husband, one of King Clifford's soldiers.

"Prince Paul has been very rude about King Rudolf
from the next kingdom," the cook called to her husband.
"King Rudolf is sure to be very angry. He will send his men
to seize our Prince and lock him up in the dungeon."

The soldier looked worried and ran to tell his captain.

The captain immediately called out the guard.

"Men! That ruffian, King Rudolf, is sending troops to seize Prince Paul and lock him in the dungeon."

The guards mounted the battlements of the castle, armed with their muskets.

How fierce they looked! They stared across the valley,
looking for any movement that might mean the start of war.

Meanwhile, across the valley in the other castle,
good King Rudolf, unaware of what was going on,
was eating a particularly tasty kipper for his afternoon snack.

"Yum, yum," he said. "These kippers are particularly tasty.
I think I'll send one to my very best friend, King Clifford."

He called for the royal messenger.

The messenger set off for King Clifford's castle,
carefully carrying a particularly tasty kipper.

As he approached the castle,
he suddenly saw the battlements crammed with soldiers,
their muskets pointing across the valley.

"Thundering cannon balls!" he cried.
"I must warn the castle guards."

He turned his horse and galloped back the way he had come.

When he arrived back at King Rudolf's castle,
he shouted to the captain:

"That cowardly custard, King Clifford, is about to attack.
Call out the guard!"

As fast as they could, the soldiers mounted the battlements,
muskets at the ready, waiting for the first sign of battle . . .

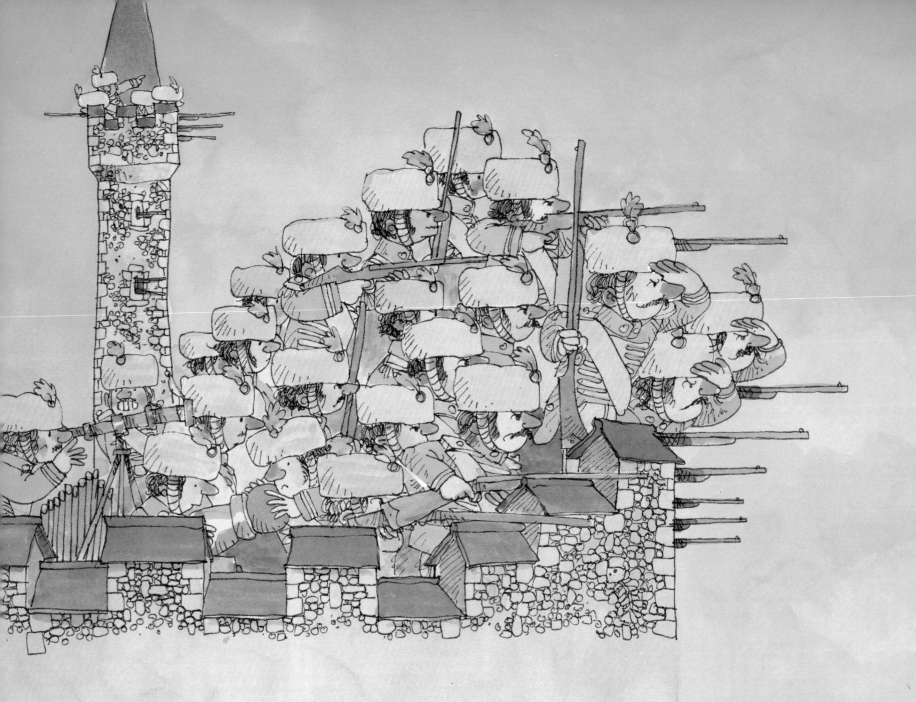

The soldiers of King Clifford, muskets at the ready,
stared across the valley from their battlements
to the castle of King Rudolf . . .

The soldiers of King Rudolf, muskets at the ready, stared back across the valley from their battlements to the castle of King Clifford.

Both waited for the other side to make the first move.

They stood there bravely all through the night . . .

The next morning, Prince Paul woke early.
After breakfast, as it was not quite time for school, he decided
to go and talk to Jim, who was the son of the castle cook.

They were good friends.

As he reached the kitchen, some soldiers who had spent
all night on the battlements were having their breakfast.
They looked cold and miserable.

"Good morning, Jim," said the Prince.

"Good morning, Prince Paul," said Jim.
"I hear that you have been to school
and that you have written a letter."

"Yes," replied the Prince.
"It was a very difficult letter to write."

"I can believe that," said Jim.
"It has caused a terrible fuss in the castle.
Everyone is talking about it,
but no one will tell me what you wrote."

Prince Paul looked rather surprised.

"Oh," he said. "I wonder why?
I have to go to school now, Jim. Goodbye."

The Prince made his way to the door.

"Before you go," begged Jim,
"please, tell me what you wrote."

"Well," said Prince Paul proudly.

"Yesterday I wrote a letter 'a'.
And today I am going
to learn how to write a letter 'b'."

"A letter 'a'?" echoed Jim.

His jaw dropped open and he began to laugh . . .

The secret of the letter spread
like wildfire across the valley.
The mountains shook to the laughter
of the peaceful people in the two kingdoms.

But nobody could explain
how they had come so close to war.

Can you?

The End